Charlton

Songs of the Year

and other poems

Charlton

Songs of the Year
and other poems

ISBN/EAN: 9783337266615

Printed in Europe, USA, Canada, Australia, Japan

Cover: Foto ©Andreas Hilbeck / pixelio.de

More available books at **www.hansebooks.com**

AND OTHER POEMS

BY

"CHARLTON"

CINCINNATI
ROBERT CLARKE & CO., PRINTERS
1875

CONTENTS.

(iii)

Father, where art thou? Can no voice from thee
Break through the silence and come down to me?
Father!—that sacred name I've written here
That thou, who dwellest afar, may seem more near:
If thou couldst speak, not all the praises won
From mortal lips were sweet as thy " well done!"
These first-fruits of my song I bring to thee
In silence—yet I know thou seest me.

(vii)

SONGS OF THE YEAR.

IN a far and western country
'Neath an opal-heartéd sky,
Where the strange and glowing foliage
Takes a deeper tinct and dye,
Forth into the primal forest
Went a joyous village band,
And their songs are blown back to us
From that happy sunset land.

(9)

[First sang a woman who had drained
  The cup of life till youth had waned,
  And hope was dead, and night was near,
  The saddest song of all the year.]

I.

THE SONG OF MEMORY.

Methought I heard a still small voice
Cry to earth, Rejoice, rejoice,
Over the winter cold and dark;
Hope has drifted like the ark,
And spring has brought the first green leaf—
Forerunner of the gathered sheaf!
And then methought I heard a sigh,
It seemed the wind that glided by:
The flowers are fed with sun and rain,
But can they bring to life again
The rose that bloomed and died last year,
Or paint the leaf that's brown and sere?
The flowers will never bloom again,
For them the spring returns in vain!

[A lover sang the song of May,
The trysting time of all the year,
When all things love, and woo, and mate :
And all the village paused to hear.]

II.

THE SONG OF LOVE.

Methought her eyes were bluer
Than the sky on summer eves ;
Her voice methought made music
Like the rustling wind-swept leaves !

She touched me with her white hand
And it thrilled me through and through,
I kissed her lips and thought them
Like violets steeped in dew !

A nightingale was singing
All night to the moon's pale face ;
It seemed like the voice of our passion
Or the soul of that beautiful place !

[Then a soldier sang of battles
    And of comrades long at rest;
Standing with an empty coat-sleeve
    Meekly crossed above his breast:
Other sign was none of glory,
    For when war's alarums cease,
Freedom's mighty host disbanded
    Turn into the paths of peace.]

III.

THE SONG OF THE HEALER.

Are these the hills that trembled
    Beneath the shock of war:
Are these the vales that drank in
    Our fallen heroes gore?

How few the scars and gashes
    Upon sweet nature's face:
The springs have come and gone here
    And left their tender grace;

So like a human anguish
That leaves a holy calm.
The hills all clothed in silence
Are nature's voiceless psalm :

Save where : upon the hillsides
Open to wind and sun ;
Where silence keeps her watches
And mountain brooklets run,

Where wild clematis blossoms
And purple violets hide ;
The conquerors and the conquered
Are lying side by side :

The stars sing on together
Beyond our human ken,
And earth gives back the echo,
"Peace and good will to men !"

[Then one aweary grown
Of love, made thus his moan.]

IV.

THE SONG OF THE ROSE.

O love, love, love,
Thou art fair as the blossoming rose,
But thy beauty, and thy fragrance
With the fallen rose leaf goes;
One day in the summer sunshine,
One hour of the morning dew,
One night all steeped in silence,
And when dawn breaks anew
The memory of thy beauty
Upon the fragrant air,
But scattered are the rose leaves
And the ravished bough is bare!

———

[Then, standing in the morning light
Among her children, tall and white,
A noble matron large and fair,
With calm blue eyes, and yellow hair,
Full in her prime, sang sweet and strong
In mellow tones the harvest song.]

V.

THE HARVEST SONG.

Bring home, bring home the loaded wain
Piled with the fragrant yellow grain,
In triumph bring the harvest spoil
The fruit of all our hope and toil:
We sowed the seed with generous hand
And God has blessed the faithful land;
He sent the sun, and latter rain,
Bring home, bring home the harvest wain!

But many a flower of brightest hue
Fed by the sun, the wind, the dew,
Blue as the sky, red as the morn,

Is blooming 'mid the tasseled corn.
Thus if in hope and patient toil
We sow the seed and till the soil,
The flowers in our wheat are strewn,
We gather more than we have sown !

Soon where there is no grief or sin
My days will all be gathered in ;
But I have left the seed behind
Of others lives for sun and wind,
And winter snows and summer showers,
To ripen into fruit and flowers,
For all the coming harvest fields
Till death to time his sickle yields !

———

[Then two together sing
With voice alternating :]

VI.

THE CLOVER SONG.

FIRST VOICE.

As the bee to the blossom
So I to thy bosom
From roving and roving return :
He roves for an hour,
Then back to the flower
To drink from its honey-filled urn !

SECOND VOICE.

The bee, O my lover,
Returns to the clover,
But the blossom is withered and dead :
So thou from another
Returnest false lover,
But the bloom of my passion is fled !

[Then sang sweet nature's poet-priest,
Who holds divine the very least
Atom of dust, and yet would lay
All things in his nice scales and weigh
The worlds, as merchants weigh out gold :
Whom prudent men deem over bold.]

VII.

THE SONG OF DEATH.

The year is dying like a king in purple robes and
  golden haze ;
His weary limbs and aching brows upon our mother
  earth he lays.

Le roi est mort : vive le roi! the herald winds of
  autumn ring
Adown the echoing forest aisles unleafing for the
  far off spring.

For nature is not dead; but sleeps: already 'neath
  the purple glow
The buds are forming that will bloom beyond the
  winter and the snow.

————

[When rose among them tall and grand
He on whose breast the years had broken,
There fell upon that listening band
Silence, as though a seer had spoken.]

VIII.

THE SONG OF HOPE.

There has come to the sad old year a memory of
  the spring :
And a bird in a leafless tree-top begins once more
  to sing.

For a hazy Indian summer has fallen on the scene,
And a smile steals o'er the landscape like a thought
    of what has been.

Oh the sweet and solemn beauty of that tardy after-
    glow,
When the year is growing weary, and his pulse is
    beating slow !

Is it memory's lingering smile that softens his old
    face so,
Or the light of the coming life from the spring be-
    yond the snow?

———

[The graybeard then turned to a little maid
  Who sought the four-leafed clover at his side,
  Laid on her curls his thin white hand and said,
"And have you then no song for Christmas-tide?"
  The little maid lifted her blue eyes bright
  And singing turned her sweet face to the light.]

IX.

THE CHRISTMAS SONG.

CHILD.

Christmas bells, Christmas bells,
What is it your music tells,

Ringing out above the snow,
Ringing round the wide world so?

BELL.

Little child :—with brazen tongue
Through the ages we have rung

Every year the blesséd chime
At the merry Christmas time.

Once in holy Galilee
There was born a child like thee :

In a manger he was laid,
Roughly cradled—little maid:

But the Magi from afar
Saw the glowing eastern star,

Knelt before him and adored,
Called him Jesu, Christ, the Lord!

This is what the clappers tell
Swinging in each brazen bell,

Ringing round the world so wide,
" Christ was born at Christmas-tide !"

———

[Then one who stood among the crowd,
A poet broad and noble-browed,
Before whose eyes all space and time
Move in their pageantry sublime.]

X.

THE MARRIAGE SONG.

Yea all things come and all things go, but earth
    abideth still for aye.
In silence clothed she walks the ether realms,
    bride of the god of day;

Born of the sun, she bears the years, and feeds
    them from her own white breast,
And rocks them on her ample lap, and then she
    hushes them to rest.

The pale moon hangs her silver lamp, to light her
    way through space by night,
Queen of the air the fair earth sleeps, and turns and
    dreams in her white light.

The worlds that roll through dark and light, sun,
    moon and stars, sing on their way,

Though all things come and all things go, in depth
   of space we live for aye!

—

[Then sang a maiden fair as any star,
  And dark and tall as eastern maidens are,
  In sweet low tones that sent their lingering thrill
  To wake the echoes sleeping in the hill.]

XI.

THE SONG OF BIRTH.

Through the silence of the midnight hour,
  From the heart of the forest tree,
A single birdlike note broke forth
  Like the flight of a soul set free.

Was it the voice of a lonely bird
  Asleep on a leafless bough,
As it dreams of its mate of the summer-time
  And the nest that is vacant now?

Or was it the rush of a spirit's wings
Through the darkened arch of night,
As it broke the bonds of its earthly thrall
And fled to the morning light?

Or was it a voice from the leafless tree
At the new year's mystic birth,
As it felt the stirring of the sap
Far down beneath the earth?

But if 't was the voice of a dreaming bird
It is still : and the downy breast
Is feeling only the pricking pain
Of a thorn in last year's nest.

And if 't was a spirit's wingéd flight
It will visit the earth no more,
And a deeper silence fills the air
Than the silence that went before.

But if 't was the moving of the sap
At the turning of the year,
I shall wait in vain till this son of time
Is laid in the old year's bier.

————

[Last the young priest, beloved of his flock,
Spake, standing on a gray and moss-grown rock,
With clear eyes gazing where from earth afar
In purple ether hung the evening star.]

XII.

THE SONG OF FAITH.

Hail! sweet approach of summer-time,
When all the earth shall smile again,
When murmuring brooks will run in rhyme
And there is music in the rain!

Fair are the noiseless winter hours
When all the earth grows strong in sleep,
But fairer far the time when flowers
Like sunshine o'er the brown earth creep.

This is the time when faith grows strong
And weeps not o'er our fleeting breath,
And hope upon the wings of morn
Soars far beyond the gates of death.
Hail! resurrection of the year,
Great type of what that day shall be,
When we shall break the bonds of fear
And comprehend eternity.

MAGDALA.

I sing the fall of Abyssinia
The fate of Theodorus, King of kings!
Where the blue Nile comes from Ethiopia
To pay his tribute to the mystic tide;
Father of waters in dark Egyptus,
Giver of life, born on untrodden heights,
Bearing forgotten graves when the North star
First set its beacon in the azure night
Of Afric's glowing climes! Whose slimy ebb
And fertile flooding of slow refluent waters,
Recorded time before the years were numbered;
Wearing the shadow of the Southern cross
'Mid the dark secrets of his troubled breast.

In Magdala, the city of the hills,
The sunny hills, King Theodorus reigned,

The heaven born, begotten of the gods,

Of Sheba's royal line, the King of kings.

His spears wrung tribute from the lesser kings,

And captives swelled the pageant of his train :

Till in a hapless year, there came a band

Of white faced strangers prying through the land,

Then Theodorus, wrathful that they thus

Unbidden came, bade all his trusty men

Bind them with chains, and from this deed there
　　　sprung

Foul desolation over all the land.

> Drink, drink for the monarch,
> The cup must be brimming
> On the breath of its fragrance
> His spirit will drift ;
> It steals through his veins like
> A goblet of sunshine,
> The spell of the wine cup
> Is subtle and swift.
> What passionate sweetness
> Is sweet as the passion,
> Of steeping one's soul in

The juice of the vine?
The river of Lethe
That 's sung by the poet,
Is only a bumper
Of generous wine.

Then through the plains the glistening banners
     flashed
And scarlet trappings glimmered in the sun,
And the loud trumpet woke the faint alarm
Of distant echoes in the purple hills.
Before the troubled eyes of dusky tribes
They passed, a vision of white warriors,
With gleaming sabres, and with nodding plumes,
And all laid siege to sunny Magdala.

The maidens are coming
With music and cymbals,
And circles of jewels
Around their brown arms;
With vestures of purple,
And orange, and azure,
That serve but to heighten
Their sinewy charms.

Their brown feet are moving
In rhythmical measure,
Their bare hands are beating
Quick time to the dance,
They reel past the throne of
Their bronze-visaged monarch
Who throws them in passing
A cynical glance.

Then signs from their number
The queen of the dancers,
Whose dark eyes are filled with
A smouldering fire;
Her bosom still heaves from
The pulse of the dance, as
She lies at the feet of
Her amorous sire.

He kisses her red lips
With African fervor,
And stills with his dark hand
The passionate throes
Of her bosom; then goes from
The palace of pleasure
To steep that same hand in
The blood of his foes.

They hurled the trembling captives down the cliff
To lie in quivering masses at its base,
And from the burnished east the birds of prey
Gathered and darkened to their reeking feast.
Forth from the walls the Abyssinians came
With bows, and spears, and all the pomp of war:
Wound down the mountain path; and at their head
The mighty monarch, Theodorus, walked,
Fronting the proud invaders of the land
With all the presence of an outlawed king.
The cruel anger gleaming in his eyes
Crouched like a panther ready for the spring.
But vain are bosoms bared to meet the foe,
'Gainst cunning engines, belching smoke and fire:
And vain are spears against a foe that stands
Beyond the wingéd arrows utmost flight.
Like some lone pine that shudders to its fall
And shakes the earth with dying majesty,
Across the path of those that spoiled the land
The mighty monarch, Theodorus, fell.

THE SONG OF THE KING'S JESTER.

Spilt is the wine of the wine cup
And empty the palaces stand,
The sound of the clashing of cymbals
Is silent throughout all the land.

The maiden who danced for the monarch,
The monarch who toyed with her hair,
Are dead, and I sit mid the ruins
A jester grown silent with care.

Weep for the fall of Abyssinia,
Mother of lands in the dawn of days,
She sits uncrowned upon the stricken hills
Her hearths made desolate, her children slain.
Where is the Queen of Sheba's sacred dust,
Where is the pomp of all her pageants now,
And where her sons who ne'er should cease to
reign !

FORT WAGNER.

"HAIL, son of man, thy advent on the earth:
    Hail myriad-timéd miracle of birth:
Immortal one, whose day is just begun,
'Twas I created thee!—all hail,. my son!"
Thus sang a mother o'er her cradled child,
Rocking the little crib; and singing smiled
'Neath the dark shadow of the northern fir,
Rejoicing that a son was born to her:
Through rolling years the babe to manhood passed
No shade of doom athwart his footsteps cast.

He was as fair as some Achæan god:
Or young Endymion sleeping on the sod,
What time Diana, coming from the chase,
Stooped down to kiss the fair unconscious face;

And as she, trembling, started from his side
Fringed eyes of troubled blue he opened wide :
There was such childlike beauty in his face,
Such marriage of soft lines with tender grace,
Such woman-purity, it did not seem
Strange that a goddess kissed him in his dream.
[O, chaste Diana, who could e'er have told
Thou wouldst have loved a man of mortal mould :
Passion e'er take possession of thy breast,
Beat in thy bosom with its wild unrest :
Thou, goddess of the vaulted realm of night,
Wouldst ever fall in this our earthly plight :
Thou feel, who art all mortal ills above,
This mortal anguish of immortal love :
And thou, O goddess of the chase, e'er know
The quivering arrow sped from Cupid's bow !]
Or more, perchance, like that fair greek, who—
     when
By prudence banished from the haunts of men ;
While all the maids the silken fabrics scan,
Seizing the hidden arms reveals himself a man.

For there was stuff as stern in this young breast,
Of mortals born and cradled in the west.
But she who formed this hero 'neath her heart,
With truer courage chose a nobler part;
Taught his young lips to prate of lofty themes,
And with high hopes inspired his baby dreams.

While with another dame in high converse
Upon the anguish of the bondman's curse,
As o'er the cradle faithful watch she kept
Where, smiling in his dreams, her infant slept;
Down her white cheek the tear of pity fell:
" I love the weak and the oppressed so well
That I would give:" she cried with kindling eye:
"Yea, this, my only son, for them to die!"
Thinking, poor mother, but to illustrate
The love she bore them for their piteous fate.
When from her lips there broke that generous cry
Could she foretell it was a prophecy:
Could she foresee those golden curls should be
Mangled and bloody by the southern sea:

Or picture, lying helpless on the ground,
That snowy form gashed o'er with many a wound!
Too oft, of noble dreamers, 'tis the doom
To sleep untimely in a hero's tomb.

War now proclaimed, to arms the stripling flies:
His days are filled with dreams of high emprise:
He trains his warriors for the coming strife
Led by the rolling drum and piercing fife.
His being thrills with generous love of fame,
He longs to hear the ages lisp his name:
Yet woman's luring eyes and pretty wiles
Oft from the path his eager step beguiles:
But one there was, still fairer than the rest,
Who stirred the dormant passion in his breast.

Worthy a hero's love, sweet womanhood,
In Anna's form revealed before him stood:
The swelling bosom which her gown confines,
Gives promise of the matron's fuller lines:
Her noble presence and her eyes proud sheen

Would grace a Roman maiden's stately mien :
A helpmeet true, a staff, a guide, a friend :
Here grace and wisdom in sweet union blend.

Whilst 'neath the roof tree of his sires he passed,
Ere hastening to the camp, perchance the last
Fleet hours with those he loved; to the wide gate,
There came a hasty messenger of state.
" We form a band of swarthy troops; and need
A man of mark these lowly ones to lead :
We lay not now on you our high command
But seek your service:—will you lead the band?"
Thus wrote the Chief: the warrior asked a day
Wherein this weighty matter he might weigh.

O who can tell the struggle of his soul !
Great drops of anguish down his forehead roll :
Oft had he dreamed of wounds, and death per-
          chance,
But death, and danger, gilded with romance;
Women should strive and poets should aspire,

To wreathe his brow, and tune for him the lyre:
But this!—O God, to be the conscious butt
Of jeering tongues, who with derision glut
Their paltry malice: and instead of fame,
To marshal bondmen whom to lead were shame!
" I can not counsel!"—thus the mother spake ·
And looking on him thought her heart would
    break.
Alone he paced through all the hours of night
Till day, returning, flushed the east with light;
Then, with a hero's mien and lofty air,
He spake, and never had he seemed so fair:
" The noble chief hath sought us for this deed,
And shall he say we failed him in his need!"
Doubt and regret are banished from his breast;
To the new task he brings a patriot's zest.

The maid he loves to bear his name consents
Ere her young lover hastens to the tents:
Through clouds and storms they catch a glimpse
    of heaven:

In haste the blessing of the church is given.
Fair is the maiden standing at his side,
Robed all in white, a hero's spotless bride:
His lips, at last, receive her trembling kiss;
Too soon must cease the rapture of their bliss:
Often he clasps her to his beating heart:
Speechless and tearless—thus the lovers part.

When to the field he led his swarthy band
The eager crowd pressed close on either hand:
There too the gracious lady of his love,
Her blue eyes dim with tears, leaned high above
O'er the stone coping, and with white hand threw,
Down on his path, a rose still wet with dew:
The blushing leaves his lips an instant pressed,
And then he placed the flower in his breast,
With sudden upward glance to where his bride
Looked down through tears of mingled grief and
　　　pride. 　　　　　　　　 .
Leading those dusky troops her lover seems
Fair as the hero of a maiden's dreams:

His golden locks by amorous breezes blown,
His head with graceful gesture backward thrown,
His war-horse moving lightly 'neath his hand;
His young voice ringing clearly in command:
She leans far out to see him to the last;
Thus from the presence of his love he passed.

Far to the southward, at the dawn of day,
The hosts of battle marshal for the fray
Where beetling Wagner frets the morning skies:
" Send the black troops:" the eager chieftain
     cries:
" To lead the van: now set them in the front
And eye of Wagner: let them bear the brunt
And heat of battle; that the world may see
If night-black hosts are worthy to be free!"
Rings on the air the cannon's loud report:
The tide of battle reddens round the fort.
Shaw, with his freedmen, leads the wild attack:
The untried troops yield and are driven back;
But he, their leader, rushes on apace:

Then pause the warriors of the meek-eyed race,
And turn, and follow, up the fearful sward
Where, o'er their path, a rain of fire is poured.
When rolled the cloud of battle from the plain
The gallant Shaw was lying 'mid the slain
Within the rebel lines : while far away
The camps of freedom to the northward lay.
—O was the glory of that little hour
Paid all too dearly, when the pride and flower
Of all our armies gave his blameless life
To prove his freedmen worthy of the strife !
The white-winged angel of the summer night
Passing o'er Wagner, shuddered in her flight ;
And when from day's return she, trembling, fled
The very sun looked palely on the dead.
They sent a band of warriors from the plain
To claim the body of the hero slain.
But he, the ribald chieftain of the fort,
Drunk with his passion hurled a fierce retort :
" He's buried with his negroes : " seeking so
A slur upon the very grave to throw.

Fame took the insult by the rebel hurled
And whispered it to all a listening world :
Men said the deed, unwittingly, was fine :
The place became an altar and a shrine :
For who could guard the hero's dust so well
As those who round his body, fighting, fell.

They carried tidings how her lover died
To her who was his six-weeks-widowed bride.
Her rich hair powdered with the snows of grief
Cast her young beauty into higher relief.
And could not mar, but only served to raise
That noble beauty far above all praise.
She seemed to stand apart among the great
Touched by communion to their lofty state ;
Like some lone priestess at a mystic fane
Rapt in the silent memories of the slain.
And though she smiled, and made no outward
        moan,
Among the living, widowed, she moved alone.

THE LAST RIDE OF THE GOOD STEED FAUGHABALLA.*

I.

YON trooper on his coal-black steed,
   The scion of a desert breed
Far famed through all that western land,
Like carvèd horse and rider stand :

His nostrils glow like coals of fire ;
His eyes are filled with battle-ire ;
The free blood coursing through his veins
Knows but one hand upon the reins ;
One yoke by Faughaballa worn ;
One master rules the desert born ;
His ears like watchful sentries stand
To catch the first word of command
   Of that low-ringing voice.

---

* Faughaballa ("clear the way") General Lytle's famous black
horse killed at Carnifex.

II.

Where death and danger lead the van
There Lytle rides the foremost man;
He lingers where the bullets hiss
As lovers' linger when they kiss:
And smiles to feel his *destrier* brave
Cleaving the battle's seething wave.
His mistress is not mortal maid,
Her tresses with the laurel braid:
She woos him with her scented breath
To win her from his rival death:
She murmurs low her lover name,
And Lytle's mistress men call Fame;—
    A maiden coy and false.

III.

" Charge!"—He gives his chafing steed the rein;
The troops move swiftly o'er the plain,
When midway on their headlong course

Death strikes the rider and his horse :
The waves of battle halt and sway
Their swift impulsion reft away :
He cheers them on ; then sways and falls :
But Faughaballa leaps the walls,
Thrice makes the circle of the fort,
With wild and loud triumphant snort. -
    Sinks to the earth a corpse.

IV.

" All honor to the noble dead ! "
The southern warriors softly said.
" No braver deed was ever done,
No laurels ever better won !"
They took the pistols from his side
As trophies of that famous ride ;
And laid the warrior to his rest
Beside the river's peaceful breast :
    Far from his western plains.

V.

Fame stood by Lytle* where he lay
All through that tinted autumn day,
Unseen save by those eyes raised wide
Pleading with her to be his bride ;
" Thy course," she murmurs, " is not run,
Columbia needs her bravest son ;
When autumn twice shall tread again
With red-foot prints the southern plain ;
When thrice for freedom thou hast bled
I 'll make my lover's marriage-bed
    Beside the stream of death !"

VI.

All through the day with shot and shell
They make their fearful vengeance tell ;
And when the dark night wraps the earth,
Before the late moon's tardy birth,

---

* General Lytle was wounded at the battles of Carnifex and
Perryville, and killed at Chickamauga.

The baffled, conquered southern host
Desert their well-defended post.
When from the dewy couch of dawn
The cloudy curtains are withdrawn,
With solemn mien and reverent tread
Across the field where sleep the dead,
Their banners riddled by the storm,
They bear their leader's shattered form
    Within the conquered fort.

FROTHINGHAM'S BALL.

IT happened the night of the Frothingham's ball;
   I went with the Bertrams : 't was late in the fall;
The music, and dancing, and laughter, and light,
And flowers, all made it a beautiful sight.

Around the great entrance were gathered about
The rabble to see the fair ladies come out :
A woman and child stood aloof from the crowd,
The face of the woman was dark and low-browed :
Yet, it must have been beautiful once, that pale face,
And she carried herself with a wild heedless grace ;
But her look of despair would have turned you to
     stone,
As she stood 'mid the chattering beggars, alone ;

(49)

Her dress which was thin was bedraggled and
    torn,
But the boy was well clad, and he seemed not base-
    born.

The butler one moment is gone from the door,
The woman glides in, and for once on that floor
'Neath the glare of the gaslight, the two extremes
    meet,
The cream of the fashion, the scum of the street.
She passes the paralyzed guests in the hall
Through the silence that falls like a spell over all,
And none lays a hand on the woman; like fate
She crosses the threshold, and then 't is too late.

Frothingham stood there full under the light,
His wife at his left hand, his boy on his right.
She entered the room and came slowly along,
With her boy by the hand, through that gaily
    dressed throng;
He started, turned red, and then pale at the sight,

And the wife of his bosom was trembling with fright.
She came where they stood, and then paused with
    the child,
And spoke in a voice that was broken and wild :

" We wandered together in darkness and night
Till we came to your house all ablaze in the light ;
He asked who was his father : and, lady, I came
To answer that question, and show you his shame :
My son, there 's your father : nay, fear not his scorn !
Yes, lady, they 're brothers, but mine 's the first-born.
See, lady, in both the same look of surprise,
The same golden curls, and the same deep blue
    eyes ;
Ah ! do you not see how the life streams that course
Through their veins, are each fed from the same
    parent source ?
But I was his mistress, and you are his wife,
And your son will live like a prince all his life,
While mine is thrust down to be one of the mob ! "
And then her voice broke in a shuddering sob ;

And she shook, and she trembled, and shivered and
    cried,
And the boy fell to sobbing, and clung to her side.
The woman he honored drew close to her lord,
While over the two her hot anger was poured;
The hearts of his guests with strange pity were
    stirred,
But he looked on the woman and spake not a word.

'T was the butler, I think, who found on his stand
The watchman, who laid not unkindly his hand
On the woman and led them away from the rooms.
"Where!" none asked, but most likely a cell in the
    Tombs.

It broke up the dancing, and each guest withdrew
With conventional phrases of formal adieu.
The dreams of the sleepers were troubled and
    stirred
With the sight they had seen, and the words they
    had heard;

But the morrow they laughed with a laughter as
    light,
And forgot the grim ghost they had seen over
    night.
You ask what became of the woman forsaken?
I remember 't was said that the father o'ertaken
With tardy repentance, the wife moved with pity,
Sought the outcasts in vain through the dens of the
    city.

They eased their remorse with the moral reflection,
That what can not be helped should not cause us
    dejection ;
And time the avenger and healer halts not,
Weeks passed, she was silent, and they too forgot.

Both were his sons, and the women had been
Each dear to his dastardly bosom, I ween ;
But one for a summer, and one for a life,
One was his mistress, and one was his wife ;
One he beguiled with the false words he told

Of altar, and priest, and a ring of pure gold.
His marriage was pledged in the same words, I
         trow,
But one was a promise, the other a vow.

'T is not often we look on this truth face to face,
And we ask not how many are wrecked in this
         place ;
We shrink from a problem so tragic and grim,
But what do you think should be meted to him
Who betrays a poor woman, and steals all the sweet
From her life, and then casts her out into the street?

THE ALCHEMIST'S DREAM.

OLD !—so old !—with his head bent low,
And the heart in his bosom beating slow:

By the gleam of the taper's flickering light
The alchemist toiled through the hours of night.

He brought strange herbs from distant lands
And mingled them all with his trembling hands,

And sought the secret of life in vain
That should touch his locks to gold again;

Softly he smiled at his midnight toil
And whispered : " The miser may seek to spoil

" The earth, in search of her secret old
To fill his coffers with yellow gold.

" I seek the clue to a deeper truth,
The mystery of undying youth."

Often he mingled the potion again
And wrought the secret of life in vain.

And ever he sought in his mystic lore
Only one little ingredient more.

Once, as his midnight watch he kept,
He bowed his hoary head, and slept.

A sunbeam fell through the shadowy night
And there came to him on its path of light,

A beautiful woman, tall and fair,
With deep blue eyes, and golden hair.

She wore in her breast where the soft lines meet
A bunch of violets fresh and sweet;

As close she came to the dim oak stand,
She loosed them with her snowy hand:

And spake in tones so low 'twould seem
A zephyr breathing through his dream;

Standing beside him white and calm
Holding the violets in her palm.

"Sun, and earth, and dew, and wind
All their mystic powers combined;
Time, the alchemist, had brought
Hoarded juices, and had wrought,
Many years beneath the earth
For the hour that gave it birth;
Fanned it with the winds that blew,
Fed it with the sun and dew,
Fashioned every secret part,

Petal, stem, and golden heart,
That this little purple flower
Should but blossom for an hour:
Wrought it in a mystery,
This is nature's alchemy;
O vain mortal, would you then
In but three score years and ten,
Solve the secret of your youth,
Mix and mingle here forsooth,
In this little cup of gold,
All its mysteries manifold;
Trace the sources whence you came,
And resolve your solid frame
To rebuild it in an hour
With your earth begotten power ?
Yet, grieve not, for the mystery
You seek, is immortality,
And the violet when it dies
But returns into the skies."

He woke to find himself alone,
The lamp was out, the vision flown :

But stealing faintly through the gloom,
The scent of violets filled the room.

MIDNIGHT.

As the clock was slowly striking
 Midnight in the old oak hall,
Breathless silence fell around me,
And I heard an angel call :
All my flesh seemed growing weaker
And my spirit gaining strength,
" Come ! " the waiting angel whispered,
And I felt my wings at length.

Through the blue we sped together
Till the earth waned like a star,
And we lost her in the distance
Where the waves of silence are :
And I saw a golden radiance
Fall upon our soundless wings,

And the ether spread around us
In illuminated rings.

Saw a host upon a mountain
In a golden haze of light,
Every brow was wreathed with laurel
Every form was robed in white :
And a music softer, fainter,
Than the breeze that stirs the rose,
Round the bases of the mountain
Faintly ebbs, and softly flows.

But the angel drew me onward
To the mountain's dizzy verge,
And I looked down deep abysses
Where the waves of darkness surge :
Countless hosts of men and women,
Pale and passionless and sad,
Some were worn with hopeless watching,
Some were weeping, some were mad.

Who are these? I cried in anguish,
And my fleshless spirit quailed;
Then the angel softly answered,
" The unnumbered ones who failed:
See how vastly they outnumber
Those whom earth delights to praise,
They have borne the cross of genius
But they wear no deathless bays ! "

TO MARION.

FAREWELL, calm lakes, and tinted hills,
　　And streams that flow by murmurous mills :
And Berkshire elms that stud the vales
Where autumn plies her winnowing flails.

Yet not for these, when I am gone,
Will memory lead me by the hand
Back through the vista of the past,
Till once again I seem to stand

Within the home upon the hill—
A picture mirrored in the lake ;
Where happy sounds of laughter light
The answering hillside echoes wake.

(63)

Not for the scenes that meet the eye,
But for the thoughts that fill the heart,
For memories dear of kindly deeds,
And claspéd hands that fall apart.

There is a light upon the lake
Softer than haze by autumn shed,
A light that stays upon the hills
When autumn's mellowing sheen is fled.

It never fell on hill or vale,
'T was ne'er reflected in the lake,
Yet all the changeful scenes around
New beauty from its presence take.

Farewell, dear friends! I send you these
Weak words that half reveal my love;
God keep your home upon the hill
All earthly ills and clouds above!

THE LOST PATH.

MOUSIE tripping o'er my floor,
Coming shily to the fore,
Peering slily through the crack,
Rushing, scampering madly back;
Mousie, have you lost your way,
Have your footsteps gone astray?
Round and round my room you roam
Vainly seeking your way home:
Ah! gray mousie, trembling there,
Others know thy wild despair,
Other lives have gone astray
On a wider darker way;
In that lone and fearful hour
Storms and shadows darkly lower,
And alone they face the blast

Seeking vainly some lost past:
Mousie, like thee, far from home
All life's weary paths they roam.

LINES WRITTEN IN AN ALBUM.

L IKE unto this unwritten book
 Thy life unfolds its leaves :
Who can foretell the closing page
And who the garnered sheaves?

Then slowly read the book of life
And linger o'er the page,
For we may never turn again
The leaves from youth to age.

This is the sibyl's mystic book
Its secrets all her lore ;
And hope the flickering lamp that dies
To kindle nevermore.

ONLY.

ONLY a portrait looking down
    Upon a woman* bent and brown,
Haggard with want and bowed with years:
There's nothing, friend, to move your tears.

Only a garret dark as fate,
A bed of straw, a fireless grate,
A tattered paper on the wall,
And looking down upon them all,
With Christ and Mary on each side,
The portrait of a regicide.

Only a life that ebbs away
Dying of hunger day by day;

---

* The widow of Pietre, the regicide.

While on the wall there hangs above
This miracle of woman's love,
With Christ and Mary on each side,
The portrait of a regicide.

O love, that covers every sin,
Did ever bard or hero win,
In all this weary world beside,
Such love as this poor regicide?

FROM A WATER BABY TO CHARLES KINGSLEY.

I COME from the Pacific
  Where water babies swim,
According to Charles Kingsley's
Most scientific whim.

Like the giant of his story,
If he would read us true,
He must turn into a baby
And study us anew.

For we 're the seed of promise,
But he 's the fallen leaf,
And vain 's the coming summer
To autumn's garnered sheaf.

(70)

THE KNIGHT OF ATHOL.

A BALLAD.

O WHITER than the lilies
    That bloom beside the gate,
The lady of the castle
Awaits in silent state.
Her knight is gone with Richard
To fight for Holy Land;
The ship that should have brought him
Lies shivered on the strand.

Ah ! well the Knight of Athol
Has battled for his God,
And low lies many a Moslem
On Israel sacred sod :
His arm is strong as iron,
His heart is true as steel,

Before the Holy Altar.
He's sworn to win and kneel.

But on a glowing even,
Amidst the deadly fray,
Many a Turk had fallen
Beneath his sword that day,
Three Moslems rode down on him,
Their cimeters on high,
One struck him on the bosom,
And one across the thigh.

Ah! long the Knight of Athol
Lay bleeding unto death,
Many an hour had flitted
Before he drew his breath;
His goodly strength was broken,
His battle days were o'er,
The knights that knelt around him
He'd ride with them no more.

Through weary years there watches
A lady in her tower,
And with her beads she numbers
Each slowly passing hour :
The ship that should have brought him
Is shivered on the strand,
The gallant Knight of Athol
Will never win to land.

She builds a cloistered convent
Beside that treacherous wave,
And from her tower the abbess
Looks down upon his grave :
She watches morn and even,
She prays at noon and night,
Ah ! well I ween is resting
The soul of Athol's knight.

THE FOUNTAIN.

" A GIFT, a gift!" The city cried,
   "A gift of water purified!"
The turgid stream is raised on high
To gleam a rainbow in the sky,
And fall from lifted hands again
In benediction like the rain.
The passing traveller weary bows
And drinks and laves his aching brows,
The parched and fevered lips of pain
Drink the cool draught, and drink again,
And little children laugh and play
Within the circle of its spray :
And old and young, and rich and poor
Wash in this fountain and are pure,

And thus the giver of good gifts
This fair embodied water lifts,
And raises from the generous tide
Toward heaven, a city purified.

TO A CHILD.

POOR little rosy, tottering feet,
 They scarce can stand alone,
But they must learn a harder task
Dear feet ere they are grown !

In all life's rough and thorny paths
To stand, and walk alone :
Through all her dark and rugged ways
To pass and make no moan.

No friendly hand reached out to stay
Their steps through the unknown ;
They tread the vale of life, like death
Unguided and alone.

(76)

O would that I could stretch my hand
To thee, my child, my own ;
But thou must walk the future days
As I have walked—alone !

HER LETTER.

FAREWELL!—That I should ever write
  These bitter words to thee!
Farewell, and hope no more, my friend,
For it may never be!

Those summer days when we two loved,
How near, how far they seem;
Their golden hours have flitted past
The pageants of a dream,

'T was but an idle tear that fell
And blotted these sad lines:
Why weep that every life must hold
Its desolated shrines?

(78)

Perchance, the gentle hand of time
Will cover them with flowers,
And memory love to linger round
These broken shrines of ours:

Thy name, a silence in my life,
May one day grow to be,
Faint as the scarce-remembered strains
Of some sweet melody!

When our unsexed shadows meet
Beyond the silent shore,
Shall we two love in that strange land
Where partings are no more?

Or will the light that flooded life
With radiance divine,
Fade like the sunset's after-glow
From some deserted shrine?

I linger that I may belong
One moment more to thee,
Out of all time !—'T is over now—
Farewell !—Remember me !

THE VILLAGE MAID.

I WAS a little village maid
   Down by the wild sea shore,
Life was so sweet, and yet I longed,
I longed for something more.

Many a gallant sailor lad
Asked me to be his wife,
And yet I longed for something more
Than simple village life.

I met Lord Edward at the stile,
When all was dark above,
And yet I longed for something more,
I longed for Edward's love.

I walked beneath the village trees,
Lord Edward by my side,
And yet I longed for something more,
I longed to be his bride.

And now I hold a little child
Against my throbbing breast,
And still I long for one thing more,
I long to be at rest!

HYMN TO THE DEAD.

I.

MORTAL, turn thee to thy rest,
Fold thy hands upon thy breast,
Close thine eyes and hold thy breath
In the silent halls of death!
These white hands shall hold the palm,
These pale lips shall chant the psalm,
These still feet shall tread the shore
Where death enters nevermore!

II.

Spirit, hasten to thy rest;
Verily the dead are blest!
Thou hast died to rise again
Freed from every mortal pain:

Thou shalt wake from thy long sleep
Where tired eyes forget to weep;
Thy dull ears shall hear the chimes
Ringing in celestial climes!

A SERENADE.

OH sweet in the hazy summer-time
    Are the sounds of the forest to me,
But the sweetest of all earth's sweetest sounds
Is the sound of the moaning sea!

Then come across the sands, my love,
By the light of the evening star,
And listen to the distant wave
As it breaks on the fearful bar.

The night is all too fair, my love,
To dream away in sleep;
Then come with me to the golden sands
And look on the mystic deep!

(85)

All night the wild waves sing of love
To the moon, the sea's pale bride,
And he woos her from her lonely heights
To sleep on the breast of the tide.

TWO VISIONS.

I SAW a maiden seventeen,
　And she was passing fair;
The sun his benediction laid
Upon her golden hair.

And still beside the sunlit wave
Methinks I see her stand,
Fair as the lily that she held
Within her folded hand.

Frail as the light bark was her form
Before it meets the shuddering storm.

I saw a vision of the night
Beside the darkling lake,

And o'er the waters and the maid
The faltering moonbeams break.

And still she wanders like a wraith
By the waters cold and dark;
Love took the lily from her hand
And wrecked her fragile bark.

THE SPANISH STUDENTS.

NOT in a great and glorious cause,
    Not for their country and its laws,
But dead to fill the greedy maws
Of despotism and tyranny.
Not on the battle-plain they fell
Beneath the storms of shot and shell:
With pale, mute lips that scorned to tell
Their bitter boyish agony,

They faced the fierce and hungry crowd
So sad, so young, so calm and proud,
For one mad freak and troubled shroud
They paid the last dark penalty.
The sum of their brief days all told
Would scarce make two of them seem old,

And yet they passed so brave and bold
From life on to eternity.

Ere twice the sun had sunk to rest,
Ere they one friendly hand had pressed,
Poor boys, or on a mother's breast
Wept out their hopeless misery,
The soldiers to the public place
Led them to die : each fair young face
Was worthy of its noble race,
Fronting the Spanish musketry.

Eight youths the flower of Spain have died
That mob-rule might be satisfied ;
O Spain ! now woe to thee betide
For thy cold inhumanity :
The dead shall cry aloud to God,
Their blood shall feed the Cuban sod
Till heroes rise up vengeance shod
For their untoward destiny.

In shedding human blood ye sinned
And sowed broad-cast the wild whirlwind,
But ye shall reap again the wind
The mead of all your cruelty :
For there shall grow from each green grave
In that fair isle kissed by the wave,
The isle their martyrs died to save,
The passion-flower of liberty !

LINES

ON A SKELETON SHIP FOUND IN THE AMERICAN DESERT.

THY fleshless ribs bleach on the plain,
　O wave-forgotten ship:
How long, how long, since thou wert last
Kissed by the sea's salt lip?

Ship of the past, thou liest now
Upon a waste of sand,
Below the line upon the hills
That marks the waveless strand.

Here must have rolled some mighty sea
But whither has it fled,
To leave thee stranded thus alone
Upon its arid bed?

(92)

No sea-mew comes on feathered wing
Forerunner of the storm,
No sea-weed trails its tresses through
Thy ribbed and shrunken form.

When did the sweet winds fill thy sails
Above a murmuring sea;
Were yon far hills a tropic shore
O ship of mystery?

The earth is changed, the sea is gone,
The desert round thee lies,
And still thou liest mutely there
Beneath the burnished skies,—

Till science from the voiceless lips
Of earth her secret robs,
And lays a finger on the pulse
Of time to count its throbs.

LINES

ON THE SINKING OF THE ONEIDA.

GO forth unharmed upon the earth,
Free, as the noblest son of man !
Breathe heaven's taintless summer airs ;
Sleep even, if you can !

But look not on that smiling sea
As treacherous as thou,
Thou antitype of Cain !   Go free,
His brand upon thy brow !

Like him, unshackled wander forth
Bearing thy chainless curse !
Great Heaven, pity this lone man
Shunned by the universe !

(94)

"Am I my brother's keeper? I!"
 This echoless wild prayer`
 Rings through the blood-stained ages; 't is
 The death-cry of despair.

The flowers for him drip human blood,
 The airs are filled with ghostly moans,
 The waves that ripple on the sands
 Sound in his ears like dead men's groans.

For yonder sailor sent to death
 A hundred hero souls:
 Unloose his bands! . Let him go free!
 Heap mercy's fiery coals

Upon his pitiless craven head!
 Leave him in life's dead calm
 Like that false sea; and men go by
 Nor touch his guilty palm!

And, England, mother of the free,
Leave not thy work undone;
In justice to thy noble dead,
Disown this dastard son.

POET AND RIVER.

POET.

FAIR Innisfallen, sweet Innisfallen,
    Brightest of waters that flow,
Tell me, O tell me, hastening ever
Whither, O whither you go!

RIVER.

Whither the dreams of your boyhood have gone,
Whither your manhood will go,
Into the void of the limitless sea,
Whither the rivers all flow.

Out of the light of the sunshine we go,
Far from the flowers that bloom
And fade, on the shores we'll visit no more—
Together we haste to our doom!

(97)

Whither the waters of time flowing far
From rivers whose sources are fed
Out of the future, that deep hidden spring,
Are lost·in the days that are dead!

To the past, to the gulf of the ages,
Into the wide shoreless sea
That covers our life with its silence,
Thither I hasten with thee!

HYMN TO THE EUCHARIST.

THIS is the bread that feeds my flocks,
  And this the wine of life;
These are the holy mysteries,
The emblems of the strife.

Our Lord is risen from the cross,
No more to suffer death;
"'T is finished!" thus the dying Lord
Cried with his failing breath.

No more upon the altar now
We make our sacrifice;
These are memorial services,
His blood has paid the price.

(99)

Forever now our risen Lord
Sits at Jehovah's side,
His body shall unbroken be
And healed his bruiséd side.

IDLESSE.

FLICKY, flecky, flocky sheep,
   Standing in the grass knee-deep,
Browsing, drowsing, half asleep.

Frisking, skipping little lambs
Playing round the hornéd rams,
Bleating faintly for your dams :

Nibbling off each grassy blade ;
Huddling in the fragrant shaded
By the leafy aspen made.

O 'twere sweet to while away
All one idle summer-day
Following the shade that way !

Yea 't were passing sweet!—what though
To the shambles they must go,
Naught of this the dreamers know.

THE MARRIAGE OF THE LAMB.

ALL hail! Thou spotless bride of Christ,
Come forth to meet thy Lord!
The guests are waiting with their lamps
Wherein the oil is poured.
Around the church, his chosen bride,
The faithful virgins stand :
Kindle your lamps, the night is dark,
The bridegroom is at hand!

She comes arrayed in shining robes,
Without a seam or stain :
Within her virgin home her feet
Shall never pass again.
She enters now the bridegroom's house,

The mighty heavens above,
The mansion of the bride and groom
Whereof the light is love!

THE QUEEN OF THE WEST.

OUR blue grapes grow
    Where the waters flow,
Round the banks of the beautiful river:
Where the Queen of the West,
Her fair brows pressed
With a wreath of the graceful vine,
Lets the beams of the sun
Through her wine-cup run,
To color the sparkling wine;
Whose fame has gone
To the frozen coast,
And the south-sea's salted brine.

CHORUS.

Then drain the cup to the Queen of the West,
And dash the glass to the floor;

On the fields of death, in the wine of blood
We'll drink to our queen once more.

She sits on the hills
At the gates of the west,
And her robe is a mantle of green:
With a smile of peace
She looks to the south,
And the river flows ever between;
Kissing her feet
As he enters in,
To the land of the Queen of the West;
And westward—ho!
The river goes
With her image on his breast.

CHORUS.

Then drain the cup to the Queen of the West,
And dash the glass to the floor;
On the fields of death, in the wine of blood
We'll drink to our queen once more.

But storm and tempest
Will gather I ween
Round the brow of our beautiful queen,
And blood shall flow
In the vale below,
Where the grapes grow purple and green ;
She looks to the south
To the fields of death,
O'er the river that rolls between,
For a sea of blood shall ebb and flow
Round the feet of our beautiful queen.

CHORUS.

Then drain the cup to the Queen of the West,
And dash the glass to the floor ;
On the fields of death, in the wine of blood
We 'll drink to our queen once more.

A NIGHT PICTURE.

A YACHT sailed slowly from the south,
 And moored below my window-sill,
Under the shadow of the rock,
And furled its sails, and all was still.

The yacht's light glowing like a star
Threw flickering gleams on deck and mast;
The water lapping round her sides
Scarce broke the silence as it passed.

Upon the river's further side,
Across the heaven's azure field,
Above the mountain dark and bold
The moon lifts up her silver shield.

(108)

The yacht is in the darkness save
Her red star gleaming through the night,
One moment more, river and yacht
Are flooded with the golden light!

LINES.

SITTING alone by the cold gray wall
Where the dark-leafed creepers climb and fall :
Holding her child to her heavy breast
Where the full red lips are softly pressed,
Kissing and clinging and falling apart ;
Sending a thrill to the mother's heart,
Healing the wounds of the heart that was broken,
Of the lonely heart of the desolate woman :
Drinking the purest draught on earth,
From the fountain of love that gave him birth.
The soft round limbs that wrought her such pain,
Pledges of days that come never again :
All, all are hers, save the clustering wave
Of sun-brown curls his father gave.
Dost thou love him better, thou lonely one,

For the father's touch on thy little son?
She gives two kisses where mothers give one,
For the father who never has kissed his son :
And folds him closer within her arm
As though to shield him from shame or harm ;
But the mother's wistful drooping eyes,
Where the shadow of trouble darkly lies,
Are turned from the child so fondly clasped
With a dreamy gaze on the distant past.
On the parted lips is a smile of peace,
With a yearning look that shall never cease,
For the soft lips droop, and seem to miss
The remembered touch of the loved one's kiss :
Ah, well we know if those lips could part,
Not one harsh word from the troubled heart,
Not one rebuke would the lips have spoken
Though the mother and child are forsaken !

TO THE NEW YEAR.

I BOW, I kneel, I pray to thee,
   Dim presence veiled in night,
Reveal thy radiant form to me
Robed in effulgent light.

I send my ship of hope afloat
Upon thy tideless stream,
The old year seems already like
A faint and vanished dream.

Bring the impossible to pass
In thy resplendent lights?
On the strong wings of hope I rise
To blue untrodden heights.

(112)

I bow to thee, I kneel to thee,
Veiled prophet of my days,
Thou art so bright I can not see
Thy dark and rugged ways,

That lead through lone and sunless vales,
The paths of the new year:
I bow to thee, I kneel to thee
In mingled hope and fear!

DANTE GABRIEL ROSSETTI.

A POET'S arisen in time,
  And the rhythm of his musical rhyme
Is filled with a pity sublime;

With sorrow as pale, as pale as the moon,
And passion that glows like the noon,
And deep thoughts that fade all too soon.

What though the worn theme of his song
Be ever of woman's dark wrong,
Does not mercy to genius belong?

Pure loves are the stars that inspire,
And the poet who writes of desire
May kindle a white altar fire:

(114)

But the false singer's torch leads astray,
And its lurid gleam lightens the way
Whence none may return to the day.

THE WATER SPIRIT OF THE SAGUENAY.

DARK glance the waves beneath our feet,
  And dark the clouds on high ;
The white foam on the blackened tide
Laughs as it flashes by !

The granite walls rise grand and dark
The frothing stream beside,
They look upon the setting sun
And smile in solemn pride !

Here bathes the Syren of the stream
Within her moss-hung caves :
Her hair like molten sunlight gleams
And round her bosom waves !

(116)

Faint and sweet is the song she sings
To lure men to their death :
The river's sound is in her voice,
The wild-flowers in her breath !

Thus on life's stream some syren song
Allures man to his fate,
While echo whispers from the shore
" Too late, lost soul, too late ! "

Sing, water-nymph, thy syren song,
Set thy false beacon light;
Our good ship glides adown the stream,
Good night, sweet friend,. good night !

SUEZ.

HAIL! resurrection of nations
    That phœnix-like heavenward soar;
The nations that parted at Babel
Are building together once more.

  Hail, the clasped hands of the peoples,
The pomp and the pageant of peace;
Where hearts are laid down in the desert,
A mantle without seam or crease,

For a woman to walk in her beauty
Subduing the nations of earth,
To the cradle that rocked the young ages,
The shrine of the old world's new birth.

(118)

Does she stand as a woman who blesses
The past that flowed over this sand?
Does she stand as a woman, a prophet
Proclaiming the hour is at hand?

It is womanhood's apotheosis:
She comes with the cross in her hands;
She comes: and the rivers of plenty
Flow out through the once barren lands.

The waves of the land-girded ocean
Are flowing from India's main;
And the rock that was smitten by Moses
Is yielding its waters again.

BRIGHAM YOUNG.

THE Mormons at the bar of fate in calm defi-
    ance stand,
An outcast band of Ishmaelites in this our Christian
    land:
Grand in the borrowed dignity of courage and de-
    spair,
They turn upon their mighty foe, and front him in
    their lair,
Ere once again their wandering steps still farther
    westward fly
From the stern presence of the law's unveiléd
    majesty;
And he, their hoary patriarch, who might have
    been so great

If he had served a greater cause, falls from his
pigmy state.

These beardless patriarchs revived the hoariest sin
of time,

And bade an outraged world proclaim their travesty
sublime ;

And sought to flaunt in this fair clime where freedom holds her sway

A broken and dishonored law in the calm face of
day :

But freedom is not license, and she will not trail
her skirt,

Because she walks with lowly men, in the foul mire
and dirt ;

Nay, freedom in her garments white is perfect law
sublime,

A sword to right the lowliest wrong, and smite the
loftiest crime.

THE MART OF GOLD.

FOLLOWED by righteous anger,
  By curses, tears, and sighs,
And covered with dishonor
The mighty gold ring dies.

All in their gilded temple
The money changers stand,
And for a price they barter
Even their native land.

They lay upon this altar
Honor, and life, and truth,
And the young men leave it
Spectres of wasted youth.

(122)

"Praise God!" the chimes are ringing
From Holy Trinity,
As lightning flashes northward
The news of victory.

For Mother Church is standing
Close to the mart of gold,
Her sacred chimes are ringing
Where blood is bought and sold.

Thus in the mighty city
Mingles the wheat and chaff:
Here votaries of Crœsus
Worship the golden calf.

They take the bread of sorrow
From the widow and her child,
And the dying patriot's pension
To this altar thrice defiled.

The curses of the soldiers
As they clasp their freezing guns;
The sighs of saintly women,
The tears of little ones,

Appeal to God for vengeance;
The very stones cry out,
This shame, the people echo,
The nation shall blot out.

Ring, Trinity, ring sweetly
Your many silver chimes,
As they rang across the city
In the good old bloodless times.

We've won the last dark battle
O'er treason, south and north;
The golden temple's shattered,
The idol driven forth!

TWO VOICES.

WHEN I am gone out of this breathing world,
 Will sentient life move calmly on its way?
Or am I but a bubble of the air,
And shall I vanish like a wreath of spray
Into the depths of that mysterious deep,
Where every life is but a beauteous wave
That breaks one moment into consciousness,
Then backward shudders to its watery grave?

SECOND VOICE.

Ask not the wind from whence it blows,
Ask not thy life from whence it came:
Seek not to stay the passing wind;
Seek not to grasp thy fleeting fame!

(125)

FIRST VOICE.

Am I a torch upon the night of time
That flares around its evanescent gleam?
Or is my life unto the source of life
But as a vague and scarce remembered dream?

SECOND VOICE.

Ask not the earth why she has borne
Thy life upon her troubled breast,
But when thy little day is o'er
Turn calmly to thy peaceful rest!

FIRST VOICE.

The life from whence my being came
Knows not annihilation's breath;
I am, I can not cease to be—
And men have called a shadow death!

LA PIU GENTILE DONNA.

I HAVE a friend so far above
   Her sex, that she seems made to love :
So lithe, so supple, and so fair,
With such a winning, gracious air
E'en envy at her sight disarms
And yields allegiance to her charms :
Her sisters own her fair and true,
And pure as the new fallen dew ;
And men in her sweet presence ne'er
At woman's wiles and follies sneer,
But feel a new-born reverence
For womanhood and innocence.

I SAID TO MY LOVE:

I SAID to my love: " In the future days,
   A hundred years from now,
What will it matter that we have grieved
   And our hearts are breaking now?"

I looked in his eyes, that were filled with pain,
   And on his troubled brow:
" O! what will it matter, my love," I cried,
   "A hundred years from now?"

" When our days are canceled and told, and we
   Are sleeping—I and thou,
Will it vex the earth, in a hundred years,
   That we are troubled now?"

(128)

" I care not," he cried, " for the moving earth—
    The future's threatening brow,
  So I spend but a day with thee, my love,
    In the blesséd sunshine now ! "

" And what care I that others share
    The pang we suffer now :
  Give me the present, and come what will
    A hundred years from now ! "

WHY doth it lie so still,
    Panoplied in silence?
All the life is gone
To Jehovah's presence.

The spirit that wore this
Has laid it calmly down ;
As the king at night-fall
Lays aside his gown..

The king is still the king,
Without his purple gown :
So the crownéd spirit
Lays its mantle down,

(130)

ONLY a rose that bloomed but a day,
It lies in my hand so still and dead:
Only a rose from within whose leaves
The soul of its passionate scent has fled.

O ye who dream of a deathless fame,
And breathe out your hearts in passionate song;
And ye who rise by your giant strength
O'er the hydra-headed seething throng:

This little rose that lies in my hand
With withered leaves that bloomed but a day,
Is the emblem of all the pride and strength
Of the world when they pass away.

Its beauty withered: its passion fled:
The dreams of its singers all unknown:
Its strength a handful of scattered dust:
Its spirit—whither flown?

I CRIED, in the heat of my passionate youth,
"A love that is true can not die!"
And marveled to see on the lips of my love
A smile that was lost in a sigh.

Ah! could I foresee, love, that I too one day
Should smile at the faith of my youth,
That the bloom of my life would so wither and fade
That I too should hold it a truth—

That this passionate incense and worship of love
Is only the instinct that draws
The youth to the maid, and the bird to its mate,
The impulse of natural laws.

A thing that must die, if you give it but time,
For the pulse of the senses to calm,
Not a spirit that dwells in this temple of flesh
As holy as prayer or psalm!

(132)

ONE lightly uttered : " Love is blind,"
  Another spake with saddened smile :
" Nay, say not so, for loyal love
  That seeth all is dumb the while.

" When true love sees the loved one's shame
  The lips are still, the heart is numb,
  She sees the truth with clear sad eyes,
  But speaks no word, for love is dumb !"
                (133)

To be, that is, to dream—
　　To float across infinity of space
Like the warm breath upon a troubled glass,
To weary time one moment with our sighs,
To draw a breath amid unconsciousness,
To see the dawn between two endless nights,
To flit a shadow on the disc of life,
To pass a dream upon the night of time,
To break the silence with a cry of pain ;
To say " I am !" and then to pass away ;
This is the scope of man's exalted will !

(134)

THE singers' voices softly rise
　　In broken music to the skies :
How sad the burdened earth would be
Without its human minstrelsy ;
For, though the wheels of space and time
Ply with a harmony sublime,
'T is but the finest ear that hears
The music of the rolling spheres,
Or all the quivering atoms thrill
The depths of space that seem so still !

ENOUGH is enough, hath the proverb well
    said:
And wholesome restraint to contentment is wed.
Not vaulting ambition is like to attain
The goal of his wishes; and, therefore, 't is plain
'T were better to steer for the safe middle-course.
Many a book has been lost on a horse
Who was full of the promise pure pedigree gives,
Yet goes lame, from hard riding, as long as he
    lives.
I own I admire the swift king of the race,
But give me a cob with a good steady pace
Who will take me in peace to each day's destina-
    tion:
Yes, give me in all things a wise moderation.

(136)

THE future is an idle dream,
  And memory a tear,
The present but a breath of time,
Gone ere we know 't was here.

(137)

LORSQU 'on doit quitter ceux qu 'on aime,
Dans tous les pays, en tout lieu,
Ou ne trouve qu 'un mot suprême
Pour ce moment d 'angoisse—*adieu!*

(138)

I KNOW a man, but he's unknown to fame,
   All homely virtues cluster round his name,
To purer heights his matchless soul aspires :
He walks the earth unscathed by passion's fires ;
His manhood is not wasted in the race,
Strength in repose adds majesty to grace.
The beggars mark his calm and pitying eye,
And know before he will not pass them by ;
No pleading voice of human grief or pain
That e'er appealed to him appealed in vain :
But ask me not, " Who is the man ? " he holds
Sacred the silence that his life enfolds.

(139)

O RESTLESS soul, worn with unrest, be still!
   Hast thou not, O parched spirit, drunk thy fill;
And dost thou still, rash mortal, yearn forsooth
For the sweet waters of the springs of youth?
Ringed round with silence in the desert-zone,
Panting and weary, outcast and alone,
Canst thou not quench the thirst that tortures thee
At the cool springs of miraged memory;
Feel the soft palm that lay within thine own:
Live in the past, though all things else have flown?
Yea: 't is divine, this deathless pain, and yet
I can not slake my soul with passionate regret!

O HAST thou forgotten the walk by the river—
  The bank where we sat long ago?
O, often I hear, through the distance and silence,
The sound of that broad river's flow !

The foliage of autumn was casting its shadows --
Its bright golden gleams o'er the way ;
It seemed that our passion had caught from October
The hues of its coming decay !

WHEREFORE ?

FROM THE FRENCH OF LOUISE BERTIN.

IF death is the aim, wherefore then on the path
Sweet flowers in the hedges that border the way :
When the winds of the autumn deflower the hedge,
Why weep that its beauty is passing away?

If life is the aim, wherefore then on the path
These stones in the grasses and thorns on the bud,
That during the journey, alas ! we are doomed ·
To wet with our tears and mark with our blood?

(142)

ON THE OPENING OF AN EGYPTIAN TOMB.

UNNUMBERED ages honored this poor dust,
   'Till some sad pilgrim on the shores of time
Entered the tomb of the forgotten dead,
And with a touch dissolved its sleep sublime.

When sacrilegious hands with careless haste
Scattered the dust of its unconscious kind,
The spirit waiting to possess its form
Fled with a sigh that seemed the desert wind.

Or, was it but the fond and foolish dream
Of this poor clay ere it was laid to rest,
That it should rise out of its pictured tomb
And live again forever with the blest?

(143)

Fairer than Egypt's dream of garnered dust,
Safe from the touch of every idle hand,
This scattered dust and its long parted soul
Shall, in God's presence, re-united stand!

PALMYRA.

THE palms may wave, the palms may shed
   Their shadows o'er thy silent dead,
But thou and all thy towers lie
In leveled ruin 'neath the sky:
O vanished city of the plain,
In dreams I see thee rise again!
I see her gay and bannered walls
Flaunt the proud conqueror ere she falls:
A mirage 'neath the burnished skies,
Her fretted towers seem to rise;
A cool oasis 'mid the sand,
Shadowed with palms, she seems to stand:
But even as the city fell,
A vanished dream, a broken spell,
The mirage fades, and o'er the plain
Ruin and silence reign again!

APOSTROPHE TO FRANCE.

THE Prussian is trampling thee under his
    heel,
And the blood of thy martyrs is red on his steel!
His armies have marched from the east to the west,
And slain in their progress thy noblest and best:
Then, rise in the might of thine agony, France,
And cast off the spell of this unworthy trance!
The priest and the alien who loved not thy soil
Have parted thy garments, and made thee their
    spoil:
But the white lilies bloom in the war-stricken plains,
And the blue blood of Bayard still flows in thy
    veins:
Then rise in thine agony, shake off this trance!
And seize thine own sceptre, O down-trodden
    France!

Are thy heroes all banished or dead? and where are
The sons of Du Quesclin, Turenne, and Navarre?
Rise, Orleans, Valois, and Bourbon, drive out
The tyrant within, and the foe from without!

ALEXIS.

H AIL, Alexis, hail !
　　From near and far
Columbia hails thee,
Son of the Czar !

Not for the power,
Nor for the fame,
Nor for the glory
Of thy great name,

Echo reëchoes
From sea to sea,
Alexandrowitz,
Welcome to thee !
(148)

In our dark hour,
Russia held forth
Her royal right hand
To the great North:

For this, O, for this,
Alexis, hail!
For this our friendship
Never shall fail!

Over this broad land,
Smiling, to-day,
Wars all forgotten,
Peace holds its sway.

We, through the night of
War-stricken plains,
Broke in the darkness
Four million chains:

Thy Alexander,
Worthy to reign,
Loosed the serfs' fetters
Through his domain :

Russia, Columbia,
For this, all hail !
For this, our friendship
Never shall fail !

Russia, Columbia,
Hand laid in hand,
Through all the ages
Thus may we stand !

Winds bear the echo
Back to his shore,
Alexis, Russia,
Hail, evermore !

KAISER WILHELM.

KAISER WILHELM is come to his city again
 A conqueror home from the war,
And Germany's heroes, Von Moltke, and Roon,
And Bismarck are riding before.

The gallant old king with his grizzled mustache
Is a king of the good olden time;
The lance-bearing Uhlans are riding before,
And behind him a pageant sublime.

Unter den Linden, they're coming, they're coming,
Our Fritz and the Princes before;
Then, warriors wearing the broad cross of iron,
And bearing the trophies of war.

This, this is the army returning from conquest,
The gallant, the steadfast, the brave :
Another is camped on the field of their glory,
The cross of their faith on each grave.

And many a woman is wearing this morning
A dead hero's cross on her breast ;
And one army enters the city in triumph,
And one is forever at rest.

But the graves on her border will guard for the
        future
The way to the beautiful Rhine :
Hail, Wilhelm ! the Vaterland welcomes her heroes,
The great iron crown shall be thine !

But Wilhelm, our Kaiser, forgets not whose spirit
Is hovering over the land ;
From the pageant he goes to the tomb of Louisa,
And lays there, with reverent hand,

The trophies from France, and the crown of our
    Fathers,
Germania placed on his head :
At the tomb of his mother our Kaiser is kneeling—
Fulfilled is the dream of the dead !

WESTMINSTER.

THERE is a minster which doth strangely seem
    Not altar, arch, and lifted spire alone ;
But the calm presence of the vanished past,
The silent ages frozen into stone :
There sleep the dead with crosswise folded palms ;
In stony calm, kings, heroes, poets lie,
Touched by the power of some mysterious spell,
And so made visible to mortal eye :
While the revolving earth rolls round the sun
This grand old minster shall not pass away ;
In marble effigy and graven stone
Lives what was once but perishable clay ;
And England, here, may look upon her past
Standing, transfigured, in the light of day.

THE NOVICE.

DEAD? Did you say she's dead,
  Who was so passing fair?
Methought that death itself,
In pity, would forbear.

Nay, father! Only dead
To earth, and earth's alloys;
Dead to its dreams of love,
Dead to its living joys.

Not in the narrow house
Where all lie down to rest,
With folded palms, to wait
The risen Lord's behest,

To rise and walk with him
Upon that distant shore,
Where earth and all her pangs
Will trouble them no more !

But in the prison-house,
And in the narrow cell,
Just wide enough for one
In solitude to dwell:

For memory to sit
And dream of what has been,
Life and its hopes shut out—
Life and its tears shut in ;

And in the name of one
Who bore Christ in her womb,
To bury womanhood
Within a living tomb !

CHISELHURST,

WALK backward, and throw a cloak above
    the dead,
And lay a hand upon the lips for silence.
Whb yesterday was monarch of the world
Is but a heap of still insensate clay.
The beggar that looks on is greater now than he ;
For he is dead.   France now may go her way.
He will not wince, although she scoff at him ;
He will not come, although she call to him ;
Nor raise his hand, though she reach crowns to him.
The lust of power, and the greed of fame,
The will that swerved not, and the brain that
    schemed,
Death jarred the busy wheels, and they are still.

But with sweet compensation in her hands
Fate brings the fallen exile two who stand,
With blanching lips, and ask not is he crowned;
But dumbly gaze into each other's eyes,
Till one falls prostrate on the senseless clay,
And cries aloud, "O mother, he is dead!"

THE GOLDEN AGE.

THERE was a day when time was young,
  And earth was in its primal bloom,
And life basked in the golden light,
Unconscious of the coming gloom,

You would have said it must have been
In the far dawn of nature's day,
When earth, a new-born smiling child,
Beneath a cloudless heaven lay.

Nay, strange and wondrous to relate,
Within my memory it lies,
A garden in the dewy dawn,   .
Beneath the changeless summer skies.

I ate the bitter fruit of life,
And passed without the shining gate:
We dwell in Eden in our youth,
But, Ah! the knowledge comes too late.

O FAR! O fair! O grandly free :
    My heart, my heart turns round to thee.
I see the might of other lands,
The tottering thrones where power stands,
And feels the slowly-rising flood
Of freedom stirring in the blood
Of peoples who are still o'ercast
With the dark shadow of the past :
And crownéd monarchs stand appalled
Before the masses disenthralled.
From these, from these I turn to thee,
O blesséd nation of the free,
Sprung full-fledged from the brows of time,
His crowning work, most fair, sublime.

" UNDER THE ROSE."

WE play in the garden,
   In life's dewy morn,
When the rose that bends o'er us
Wears never a thorn :
The wee little maiden
Stands up on tiptoes,
And innocence kisses me,
"Under the rose."

The child of the garden
A maiden is grown,
Who steals through the twilight
To meet me alone ;
We murmur our passion,
But nobody knows ;

Our kisses are given still
" Under the rose."

She sleeps in the churchyard,
And I am grown gray ;
Not many illusions
Are left me to-day ;
Yet I think that the sweetest thing
Life can disclose,
Is a kiss that is stolen from
" Under the rose."

DORÉ'S PICTURE

OF CHRIST DESCENDING FROM THE PRÆTORIUM.

STILL, central, silent, down the marble way,
    Through scoffing ranks, the path of Jesus lay:
Serenely absent, down the steps he trod—
In anguish mortal, and in strength a God.
With seamless raiment falling to the ground,
And bleeding brows, with thorns in mockery
    crowned,
And lofty mien, and troubled eyes divine,
Where some unearthly triumph seems to shine;
Wrapped in a God-like trance, he passes by
The herd that mocks at him, for them to die,
For them to bear the cross that waits him there,
For them to suffer a divine despair.
Lifted above their taunting gibes and scorn,
The sinless victim passes slowly on.

(164)

IMMORTAL AND ALMIGHTY GOD.

I MMORTAL and Almighty God! to whom
    A thousand years are but as yesterday;
Look now on us who watch the sands of life,
The fleeting sands, and hear us as we pray.

We know there falls no sparrow to the earth
But thine all-seeing eye doth mark its fall;
And if thou hearest, Lord, the birds of air
And wandering beasts of prey that on thee call,

Wilt thou not hear the human cry of those
Whom thou hast made in thine own image, Lord;
When kneeling low to thee, from trembling lips
The anguished prayer of human hearts is poured?

O stay, and strike not, we beseech thee : Christ,
Intercede thou for us with offended God !
Yet, if it be thy will that this should be,
Teach us to bow submissive to the rod.

Yea, all thou doest, Lord, thy servants know
Is wisely done : and yet, and yet, we pray,
If it be possible, O gracious Lord,
Let this dark cup of anguish pass away.

PARTHENOPE.

WHERE Naples' leafless hills, divinely fair,
    Bare their brown bosoms to the azure air,
Where flows the sea like liquid sapphire o'er
Clear depths, and murmurs to the ruined shore;
The mild-eyed Greek, with Phrygian bonnet
    crowned,
His supple limbs by Latian suns imbrowned,
Roams by the alien shore, and feels again
The dream of Athens stir in every vein:
Looking on ruins none but he could raise,
" 'T was the barbarian laid them low," he says;
'Mid the light shadows of the trellised vine,
Where dusty grapes in purple clusters shine,

With smiling lips the dark-eyed maiden stands,
Gleaning the full-orbed grapes with shapely hands;
And nature all unveiled and shameless lies
'Neath the deep silence of the wide-arched skies.

I PLUCKED a flower in every land,
    And bound it in my posy;
A violet here, a lily there,
A French rose, sweet and thorny:

A sprig of rue from stricken Spain,
In English fields a daisy:
A passion-flower from the sun-kissed land
Where nature e'en grows lazy;

A morning-glory from the isle
That trembles like a lily,
Upon the ocean's boundless breast:
I bring them willy nilly;

And lay them in these leaves to pass
In perfumes faint and airy;
To haunt these pages like a ghost
Of some dead woodland fairy.

(169)

TO ELEANOR.

WHAT shall I sing to thee, Eleanor, Eleanor?
    Maidenhood sweet and fair,
With the pure proud eyes, and the fresh young lips,
And masses of tawny hair?

Shall I sing of the peoples that dwelt of old
On the shores of this shining bay:
Like an idle dream in the sleep of time
The peoples have passed away.

Nay, what care you for the storied past
On these time-forgotten slopes,
Who dwell all day in the sunny halls
Of a maiden's airy hopes:

And what care you for the singers sweet
That sang in the old days here,
When a lover's whispered word fills all
The shell of your rosy ear.

Then build your castles, and dream your dreams,
And let the dead past rest;
There is one I know who would give it all
For the heart in thy loving breast.

NAPLES, 1874.

KALAKAUA.

KING of the isles,
  Where nature smiles,
And stoops to kiss the western sea :
Of happy isles,
Where all beguiles,
Columbia turns to welcome thee.

Where in the west,
On ocean's breast,
Tremble the jewels of the sea,
In isles afar,
Where shines the star
Of eve, the people kneel to thee.

Across the sea,
The burnished sea,

He comes, the king of many isles;
From sunny strands
To sunless lands,
Where wintry nature rarely smiles.

Through all the north,
The sunless north,
Echoes a great " all hail ! " to thee,
O King ! who dwell
Where, like a shell
That holds the murmur of the sea,

Hawaii dreams,
And floats, and seems
A cloud·upon the western skies;
While in the sea,
The burnished sea,
The setting sun in splendor dies.

O FREEDOM ! sigh not for the ruined shade
    Of ivied walls, where memory loves to dwell ;
Thine be the rayless beauty of the dawn,
The light of morning breaking overhead.
The owl hoots not within thy ruined towers,
Where sits the muse, her lyre all unstrung ;
She strikes her harp beneath the western skies,
And sings a pæan to the rising sun.
Time hath not writ on thy memorial stones
The mouldering record of forgotten days ;
She stands, a maiden in the setting sun,
And beckons us to hurry on amain.
We do not gaze on lofty penciled spires
Whose network seems to fret the glowing air,
Here sweet religion walks among the fields,
And dream-like domes of beauty fill the air.
Thine be the fame of half-forgotten lore,
The dust and ruin of the storied dead,
Ours the unworn path of days unborn,
Wherein young hope with eager steps may tread.

TO CASTELAR.

DEEM not that all thy warriors were slain,
Or thou, O Castelar, hast lived in vain!
Who set the gulf between the queen uncrowned
And this, her son, by law and justice bound:
Who paved the way for this young prince to tread
In pleasant paths? Thou and thy mighty dead.
And when there yawned a fearful chasm in Spain,
Leaped like another Curtius again?
Thou, silver-tongued and unpolluted one,
Brave as the Cid, Hispagnia's deathless son.
When time unfurls her brooding wings to show
Her sweet fruitions all divinely slow,
Then shall the seed thy generous hand hath sown

Bear fruit and flower, for ages yet unknown
To pluck and eat: and like the morning star
Thy name shall shine on Spain, O sweet-lipped
    Castelar.

TRANSLATIONS.

OLD FRENCH.

BEAUTEOUS Alice rose at morn,
All her body did adorn,
Went into an orchard fair,
Flowerets five discovered there;
Made a chaplet, in that hour,
Of the roses all in flower.
O God! would you leave this dell—
You, who love me passing well?

From the Roman de la Rose.

OLD FRENCH.

THE birdling, all-embowered in green,
When he is caught and cast within
A cage, and fed with dainties rare,
And watched with love and tender care,

(177)

Sings still ; for while he lives he sings,
With joyous breast : but, if there springs
A yearning for the tangled grove,
That nature taught his breast to love,
Then round his cage the birdling flies,
Longing to reach his native skies ;
And beats about his prisoned cage,
In the great anguish of his rage,
Seeking a space the bars between,
To fly back to his bower of green.